Tua Tee and The Fun Run

Annual
FUN RUN
TODAY!

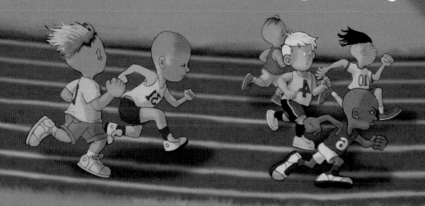

Written by Rob Buckner

Illustrated by A. Wayne Williams

Wiggle Woggle
BOOKS

Little Tua Tee was so happy this May morning. That is why he was already dressed and sitting on the side of his bed before the alarm clock went off.

The alarm clock was Tua's mom, who always opened his door and said, "Rise and shine, Tua Tee. It's time for school!"

His real name was Tua Teasley, but everyone called him Tua Tee for short. "Thanks, Mom. I have been rising and shining since five o'clock!" Tua said with a smile. "Today is the big Fun Run Day at school, and it is going to be the BEST DAY EVER!"

"I know, I know," said Tua Tee's mom. "You've been talking about it for two months now! Tell me one more time. What happens today?"
    "We get to play outside all day, eat a ton of cool snacks, and then have the Fun Run Relay Race!" Tua said with a smile.

"I know what fun is, and I know what run is, but what is a relay race?" she asked Tua.

"That's when you and a buddy run a race against the other kids at school. One of you runs the first lap around the track and tags your teammate's hand. Then, he runs the last lap. The first one across the finish line wins a gold medal and gets their picture in the school yearbook!"

"Wow! A gold medal AND a picture?" asked Tua's mom.
"Well, I don't think it's real gold! But it is a real picture!" said Tua Tee.
"Who is your buddy going to be?" she asked.
"I want to run with my best friend!" he said with a grin.

"Oh, Cooper Cash? The one you call Coop? Is he very fast?" she asked, knowing that Cooper didn't play sports and was probably the slowest kid in school.

"He's not the best RUNNER... but he's the best FRIEND ever! I think we will win for sure!"

Tua's mom knew Tua was probably the fastest kid at school, so she just smiled and said, "I know you have won a lot of races on your own… so maybe you CAN win the gold medal!"

"I sure hope so!" said Tua Tee. "Coop doesn't have any medals. He really should have one though because he's an awesome friend!"

"Well, let's eat some breakfast and get you to the Fun Run!" They finished eating, grabbed some oatmeal bars (Tua's favorite), and headed off to school. Tua Tee was so excited that he forgot to close the front door.

"Tua, did you forget something?" his mom asked.

When they got to school, some of the kids were already practicing the relays on the track. Tua wanted to hurry up and run too. He told his mom goodbye and started running to the track. He was so excited that he forgot to close the car door.

"Tua, did you forget something?" his mom asked, laughing.

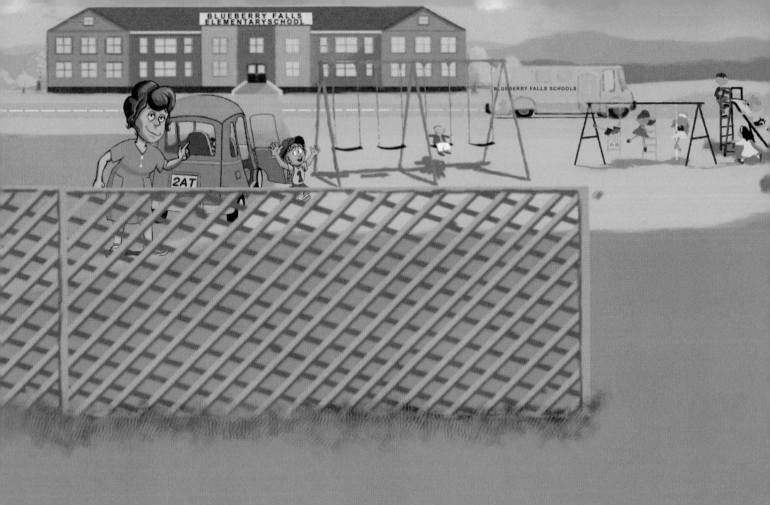

When Tua got to the track, he saw Cooper sitting with their friend Sophie on the monkey bars. "Come on, Coop. Let's do a practice run."

"I don't think I can do it today, Tua Tee.
Maybe you should get someone else," Cooper said.

"Why not?" asked Tua.

"I don't feel very fast today. You can find someone faster than me."

"No way! Me and you, we got this! Come on, let's see how fast we can run!" said Tua Tee. So, they both went over to the starting line, and the other kids lined up too. Tua told Cooper to go first, and he would run last.
"Ready… Set… Go!" Sophie yelled.
Everyone starting running as fast as they could!

Cooper was trying, but he was falling way behind. Pretty soon he was in last place, and then he fell WAY back. He started to slow down, then stopped and headed for the monkey bars again. "Don't stop, Coop! We can do this!" Tua tried to tell him.

"I'm not fast enough, Tua. You can't win with me on your team."

The bell rang and it was time for school to start, so they headed for their classroom. Tua was trying to cheer Cooper up on the way. "I believe in you, Coop! If we both do our best, I know we will have a chance to win! Please? After all, you're Super Cooper!"

"I believe you can do it too!" said Sophie with a great big grin.
"Okay, I'll try it again later," Cooper said.
"Just always do your best because the best will always do. That's what my dad always says," Tua Tee said with a smile.

So, they went through the day playing outside and eating all the cool snacks. They had grapes, granola, Jell-O pops, bananas, and the one Tua Tee liked the best, oatmeal bars! Then it was time for the Fun Run Relay Race. EVERYBODY was heading to the track to watch the big race.

Cooper was very nervous. "I don't think I can do it, Tua."

"I don't THINK you can either, Coop... I KNOW you can! As long as you don't give up. Keep running no matter what! Remember, do your best! Sophie will be cheering for us, and I will be waiting for you to tag me for the last lap!" said Tua Tee.

The teammates who were running the first lap lined up at the starting line. Coop was there with all the other runners. He looked at Tua Tee, who gave him a huge grin and a BIG thumbs up.

"Ready... Set... GO!!!!" Mr. Smart, the gym teacher, yelled.
They all started running!

Coop was trying so hard, but he was falling behind again. He kept running but was still in last place. He thought about pretending like his leg hurt and maybe limping to the monkey bars. He looked at Tua Tee and thought he would look sad and disappointed.

But Tua was still grinning and now had BOTH thumbs way up in the air!
   "You got this, buddy!" Tua Tee yelled.
Coop put his head down and gave it all he had. If he lost, he was going to lose doing his best. He was starting to make up a little ground. He was still in last place but was getting closer to the next runner. As he came around the last turn, he was almost even with him! It was getting close to the last lap and time to tag Tua.

As Coop got close to Tua, he was neck and neck with the second-to-last runner. At the last second, he gave it all he had and stretched out as far as he could. He leaned forward and tagged Tua Tee just a tad behind the runner ahead of him.

"Great job, Coop!" Tua Tee yelled as he took off like THE FLASH from their favorite comic book. He was running like a supercharged rocket and started gaining on the other runners.

Sophie jumped up and down and yelled, "Run, Tua! Run!"

He quickly passed one kid… then two… then three… and four. He was in fifth place halfway around the track. One of the four kids ahead of Tua tried to get in front of him to stop him from passing, but Tua Tee slipped around the other side. Now he was in fourth place. He kept running hard, and now there was less than half of the race left to go!

Two of the runners in front of him were running side by side. He could not get around them, so he acted like he was going to the inside of the track. The runner on the inside tried to move over to block him. When he did, Tua went right between the two runners and sailed into second place! Only one runner to beat, but not much time left to catch him!

Tua Tee was still several feet behind and the race was almost over. He was putting all he had in it. It didn't matter that he had won medals for himself before, he wanted to win this one more than any other race. This one was for Coop.

There was only a little time left and Tua was still gaining on the leader. They were both running hard but Tua was just about to pass him!

Tua Tee could see the finish line straight ahead, only a few feet away. He was now just a split second behind, but time was running out! He had done his best, but it looked like he would come up one foot short. He looked at Coop waiting across the finish line as the whole school was cheering along with Sophie. Mr. Smart was standing there holding the gold medals. At the last second, Tua Tee gave one last push and leaned his body forward with everything he had!

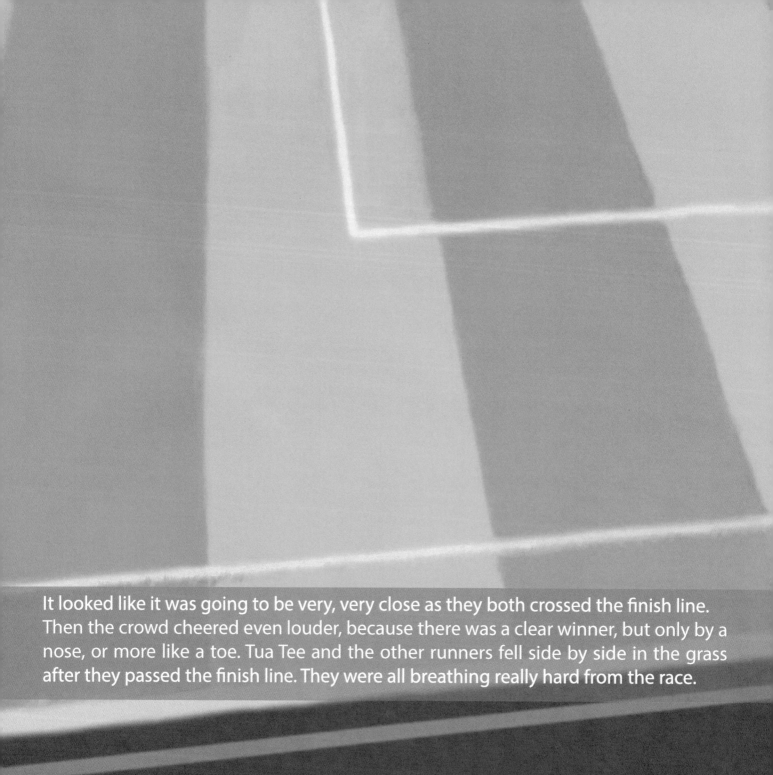

It looked like it was going to be very, very close as they both crossed the finish line. Then the crowd cheered even louder, because there was a clear winner, but only by a nose, or more like a toe. Tua Tee and the other runners fell side by side in the grass after they passed the finish line. They were all breathing really hard from the race.

Mr. Smart ran over to them and helped them up at the same time. Then he lifted one of their arms up into the air and said, "Congratulations to the gold medal winners, Tua Teasley and Super Cooper Cash!"

Coop ran over to Tua Tee, and Mr. Smart raised his arm up along with Tua's.

He then placed the gold medals around their necks. The whole school clapped and cheered for the two winners of the Fun Run Relay Race. Sophie was still jumping up and down as the school yearbook person came over and took their picture.
She didn't have to ask them to smile. Tua Tee had never seen Cooper SO happy!

Coop went over to Tua Tee's house that night for supper. They were both wearing their gold medals. Tua's mom was very happy for them. "So, how did you boys do it?" she asked.

"Coop ran so hard and kept us in the race," said Tua Tee.

"Tua Tee ran the hardest and gave it everything he had for us to win," Cooper said with the biggest smile.

The boys were both beaming. They were so proud of their victory. It took every step and every ounce of their energy to win. "You see, Mom, Coop tried his best, and I tried my best, and together, we did have the BEST day ever!"

This book is dedicated to the amazing power of friendship… and to all those who aren't the fastest, or the strongest, or even the tallest. Just be the best that you can be!

Tua Tee and The Fun Run

Written by Rob Buckner

Illustrated by A. Wayne Williams

Published by Wiggle Woggle Books

Paperback ISBN : 9798218104108
Hardcover ISBN : 9798218107222

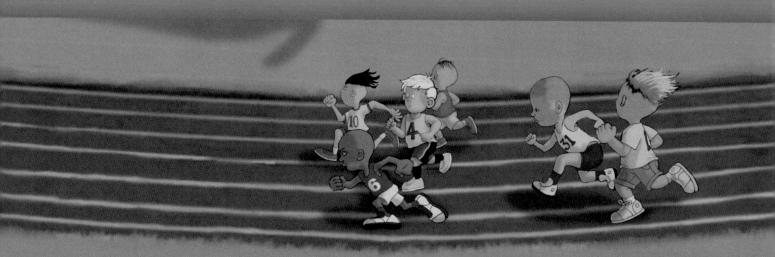

Made in the USA
Middletown, DE
27 November 2022

16187414R00027